TOP SECRET SCIENCE IN
SPACE

Honor Head

WWW.CRABTREEBOOKS.COM

TOP SECRET SCIENCE

Author: Honor Head

Editors: Sarah Eason and Petrice Custance

Proofreader: Sally Scrivener, Tracey Kelly, and Wendy Scavuzzo

Editorial director: Kathy Middleton

Design: Jeni Child

Cover design: Paul Myerscough and Jeni Child

Photo research: Rachel Blount

Production coordinator and prepress technician: Ken Wright

Print coordinator: Katherine Berti

Consultant: David Hawksett

Produced for Crabtree Publishing by Calcium Creative

Photo Credits:

t=Top, tr=Top Right, tl=Top Left

Inside: Flickr: NASA/Cory Huston: p. 30; NASA: NASA Haughton-Mars Project 2011/Mojave Field Test/Kira Lorber: p. 31t; Orion Span: pp. 32–33t, 45; Rocket Lab: pp. 22–23; Shutterstock: Adike: p. 19; Asetta: p. 5; Oliver Denker: p. 41b; DM7: p. 43; E71lena: p. 26; Edobric: pp. 3, 23t; Paul Fleet: p. 38; FrameStockFootages: pp. 40–41t; Mr. James Kelley: p. 42; KREML: p. 13r; Naeblys: p. 34; OlgaReukova: p. 27b; Sdecoret: pp. 10–11; SergeyDV: p. 39; Tyler W. Stipp: p. 18; Suzi44: p. 40b; TonelloPhotography: p. 14; U.S. Air Force: NASA/ Bill Inglais: pp. 20–21; Wikimedia Commons: Cliff: p. 9; Charlie Duke: p. 8; ESO: p 7b; NASA: pp. 1, 4, 6–7t, 27t, 28–29t, 28–29b, 35, 36, 37; NASA/Marshall Space Flight Center: pp. 16–17, 21b, 44; National Reconnaissance Office: pp. 12–13; David James Paquin: p. 17t; Ronrosano: p. 32b; SpaceX: pp. 11tr, 24–25, 25t; U. S. Army photo by Sgt. Timothy Kingston: p. 15.

Cover: Shutterstock: Adike.

Library and Archives Canada Cataloguing in Publication

Head, Honor, author
    Top secret science in space / Honor Head.

(Top secret science)
Includes index.
Issued in print and electronic formats.
ISBN 978-0-7787-5996-6 (hardcover).--
ISBN 978-0-7787-6034-4 (softcover).--
ISBN 978-1-4271-2245-2 (HTML)

    1. Space sciences--Juvenile literature. 2. Outer space--Exploration--Juvenile literature. 3. Space race--Juvenile literature. I. Title.

QB500.22.H433 2019   j520   C2018-905664-9
                                                                   C2018-905665-7

Library of Congress Cataloging-in-Publication Data

Names: Head, Honor, author.
Title: Top secret science in space / Honor Head.
Description: New York, New York : Crabtree Publishing, [2019] | Series: Top secret science | Includes index.
Identifiers: LCCN 2018053420 (print) | LCCN 2018055197 (ebook) | ISBN 9781427122452 (Electronic) | ISBN 9780778759966 (hardcover : alk. paper) | ISBN 9780778760344 (pbk. : alk. paper)
Subjects: LCSH: Space race--Juvenile literature. | Astronautics--History--Juvenile literature. | Outer space--Exploration--Juvenile literature.
Classification: LCC TL788.5 (ebook) | LCC TL788.5 .H43 2019 (print) | DDC 629.409--dc23
LC record available at https://lccn.loc.gov/2018053420

Crabtree Publishing Company

www.crabtreebooks.com   1-800-387-7650   Printed in the U.S.A./042019/CG20190215

Copyright © 2019 CRABTREE PUBLISHING COMPANY. All rights reserved. No part of this publication may be reproduced, stored in a retrieval system or be transmitted in any form or by any means, electronic, mechanical, photocopying, recording, or otherwise, without the prior written permission of Crabtree Publishing Company.

Published in Canada
Crabtree Publishing
616 Welland Ave.
St. Catharines, ON
L2M 5V6

Published in the United States
Crabtree Publishing
PMB 59051
350 Fifth Avenue, 59th Floor
New York, NY 10118

Published in the United Kingdom
Crabtree Publishing
Maritime House
Basin Road North, Hove
BN41 1WR

Published in Australia
Crabtree Publishing
Unit 3 – 5 Currumbin Court
Capalaba
QLD 4157

CONTENTS

Chapter 1: **Race for Space**   4
Chapter 2: **Eyes in the Sky**   12
Chapter 3: **Risks and Rewards**   20
Chapter 4: **The Future Is Now**   28
Chapter 5: **Living in Space**   34
Chapter 6: **What Next?**   40

Be a Space Explorer   44
Glossary   46
Learning More   47
Index and About the Author   48

CHAPTER 1

RACE FOR SPACE

Ever since humans first gazed up at the stars, they have wanted to explore the vast darkness beyond Earth. When space exploration began in 1957, it was dominated by two countries—the United States and Russia. Today, many countries around the world have joined the race for space, and private companies are planning space vacations and trips for space tourists in the near future.

GIANTS OF SPACE TRAVEL

When the United States and Russia (then known as the Soviet Union and the USSR) launched their first space missions, many failed, but the race was on to be the first country to reach the Moon. Both countries poured vast sums of money into their space programs, launching one **unmanned** space mission after another. These were craft sent into space to gather information without any crew onboard. After that, the race was on to be the first country to send a human into space.

ANIMALS IN SPACE

One of the problems that both the United States and Russia had to figure out was how a human would cope in space where you do not feel the effect of Earth's **gravity**. Both countries chose to experiment using animals, such as chimps, monkeys, rabbits, and mice. **Electrodes** were placed under the skin of the animals to **monitor** their heartbeat and breathing. Many of them died in space or on **reentry** into Earth's **atmosphere**.

SECRET EXPERIMENTS

The experiments on animals were mostly kept a secret at the time because the governments thought that the suffering of the animals would outrage the public. Recent reports have revealed that some of the "training" that was given to space animals, such as dogs, included being kept in smaller and smaller cages to get them used to small spaces.

Ham was the first chimpanzee to be sent into space in January 1961. He returned to Earth safely.

DARK SCIENCE SECRETS

Laika, a stray dog taken from the streets of Russia, became the first living creature to be sent into **orbit** in November 1957. She died in flight. Russian officials claimed that she had died painlessly from natural causes in orbit. However, a recent report claims that she died of panic and overheating just a few hours after the rocket took off. The report also states that she was put in a metal carrier inside the rocket cabin, so that her body would not turn around in the weightless environment.

This is a statue of Laika at the space training center in Star City, Russia.

RISE OF AEROSPACE COMPANIES

At the start, the Space Race was between the United States' government-backed organization—the National Aeronautics and Space Administration (NASA)—and the Russian government, using specialist equipment and knowledge that was kept top secret. Today, digital technology has made some individuals rich enough to be able to set up their own **aerospace companies**. These are businesses that have the huge sums of money needed to build rockets and spacecraft and to fund research. In addition, many engineering companies are now developing their own space technology, which they can sell to government space agencies and aerospace companies.

This CRS-8 is a craft developed by SpaceX to carry supplies to the **International Space Station (ISS)**.

FIERCE COMPETITION

Aerospace companies such as SpaceX, Blue Origin, Virgin Galactic, Boeing, Lockheed Martin, and others are employing top space scientists and investing in the latest space technology. Companies leading in the field of space exploration can make a lot of money in areas such as mining for metals on **asteroids** and the Moon, and organizing space vacations. This could include a trip into orbit just above Earth's atmosphere or a long journey to Mars. The competition is fierce, and technology breakthroughs in research and development are closely guarded secrets.

SELLING SECRETS

The race for space is big business, and so is the risk that ideas from one company may be stolen and sold to a rival organization. In some cases, an employee at one company may be paid to sell trade secrets to another company or spy for another company, or computers may be hacked and information downloaded. Much of the research and development into space exploration is also linked to the **military** and the safety of nations. More and more, governments have started to use **satellites** in space to control and manage **national security** to keep their country safe from enemy attack.

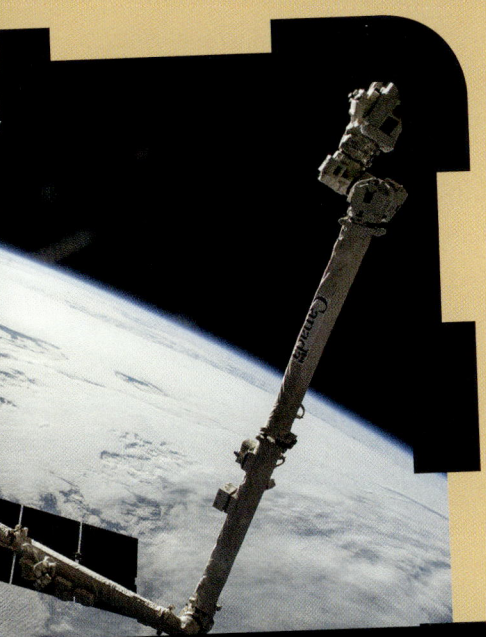

TOMORROW'S SECRETS

Asteroids, or Near-Earth Objects (NEOs), have been called "flying gold mines in outer space." One asteroid measuring 3,000 feet (914 m) across was said to contain valuable metals, such as gold and silver, worth about $5.4 trillion! Asteroids can be mined for their metals, or they can be used as bases from which to launch missions to explore deeper into space. Either way, asteroids can make companies and governments very rich. Companies are now planning how best to stake a claim on these gold mines. Lawyers and governments are creating laws to establish who owns what in outer space.

Asteroids contain metals such as tin and zinc. Although we mine these on Earth, one day we will run out of them, which is why asteroids will be so valuable in the future.

FLY THE FLAG

When Neil Armstrong and Buzz Aldrin landed on the Moon in 1969 and placed an American flag in the Moon's dust, the discussion about who "owns" space began. At that time, there were just two top space nations—the United States and the Soviet Union. There are many more countries now. Since then, China, Japan, and India have all sent missions to the Moon and Mars, and many other countries are investing money in space programs all the time.

In 1972, astronaut John Young gave a jump on the Moon next to the American flag. Behind the flag is a lunar rover vehicle.

WHO CONTROLS SPACE?

At the moment no country controls space. However, several countries are racing to mine asteroids, more and more satellites are being sent into space, and private companies are aiming to set up human **colonies** in space. Governments have a lot more competition in the race to control territory in space. Some international laws were created in the 1950s and '60s for the peaceful use of space. Other laws were added later for countries to cooperate on international space stations. New laws will be needed as private companies set up in space.

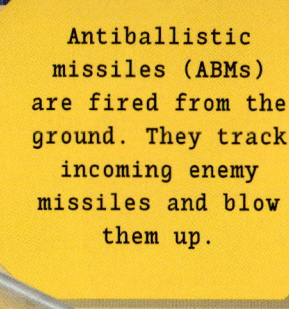

Antiballistic missiles (ABMs) are fired from the ground. They track incoming enemy missiles and blow them up.

DARK SCIENCE SECRETS

In 1983, the President of the United States, Ronald Reagan, announced the Strategic Defense Initiative (SDI). This was a proposed missile defense program that could keep **nuclear** weapons from reaching the United States. It was announced that the program had satellites and battle stations that could fire **lasers** and **ABMs** to destroy enemy missiles approaching the United States from the Soviet Union.

In 1984, as a show of strength, the United States launched two missiles in a test run. The first missile was sent from a base in California. It hit and destroyed the second missile, which was traveling at a speed of 15,000 miles per hour (24,140 kph). The two collided over the ocean in a mighty explosion. Shortly afterward, the Soviet Union cut back spending on its nuclear defense.

Years later, leaked reports showed that the "successful" test had been rigged after earlier tests had failed to hit their targets. The rigged missiles were secretly fitted with electronic devices to guarantee that they would meet in space. This display of American military power along with the crumbling Soviet economy helped bring about the end of the Cold War.

SPACE WARS

If there are no legal agreements between governments about who owns space, serious wars for the control of space could develop in the future. This could happen in the same way that countries fought for control over lands and seas on Earth in the past (and still do). Space satellites can be used for military and spying purposes, so individual governments want control over the space above their country. The greater the area of space a government or company has control over, the more powerful they could become. For private companies, space ownership could be important financially. For example, two or more companies could claim they own an asteroid that contains valuable minerals because they were the first to grab it. But which will have "legal" ownership?

MILITARY POWER

Owning or controlling areas in space can mean military power for the nation involved. With advances in technology being made all the time, the possibility of developing a defense program such as the SDI becomes increasingly more likely. The U.S. government believes that China and Russia are developing space warfare technology such as **electronic jammers** and **signal scramblers**, which block signals from satellites, making them useless. These could block signals from crucial satellites that could put the nation's safety at risk. It is highly likely that the United States and possibly other nations are looking at ways to increase their military space power in secret.

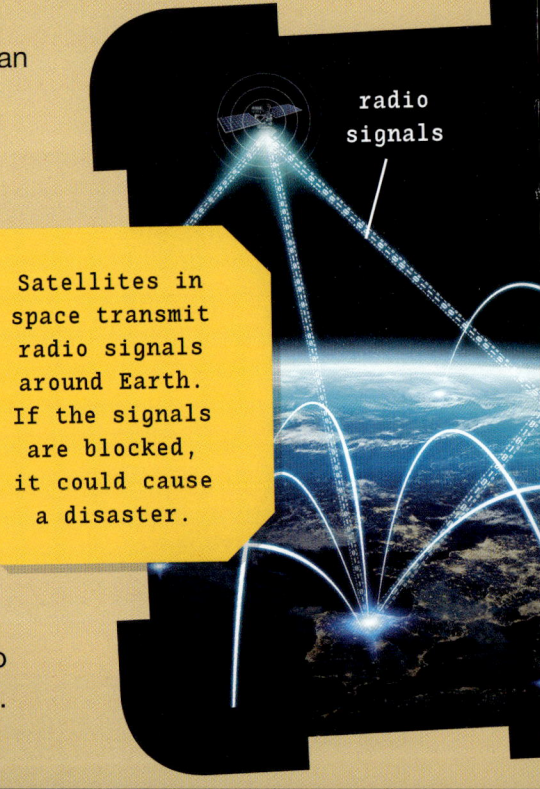

radio signals

Satellites in space transmit radio signals around Earth. If the signals are blocked, it could cause a disaster.

ZUMA SECRET ROCKET

In 2018, aerospace company SpaceX launched a rocket from the Kennedy Space Center in Florida. SpaceX streamed the launch live—but cut it off just as the rocket separated from its **payload**, or cargo. All that was revealed was that the spacecraft was called Zuma and that it had been built for the U.S. government. Government payloads being sent into space are often kept secret. This is usually because they are to do with national security, such as spying or defense.

When Zuma launched into space, it was carrying a secret cargo for the U.S. government.

satellite

DARK SCIENCE SECRETS

In 2009, an engineer named Greg Chung who worked for the aerospace company, Boeing, was arrested in the United States. He was charged with selling top secret information to the Chinese government on space shuttle and satellite developments. The court decided that his actions not only robbed Boeing of valuable trade secrets, but they also threatened the national security of the United States. Chung was sentenced to 15 years in prison.

CHAPTER 2

EYES IN THE SKY

The skies just beyond Earth's atmosphere are teeming with more than 2,000 artificial human-made satellites that orbit Earth, and this number is increasing all the time. Satellites provide us with communication information, such as television broadcasts and phone call transmissions, scientific data collection, and information used in mapmaking. They can also be used to spy, control weapons on the ground, and stop enemy missiles.

SKY SPIES

Spy satellites have been used for military purposes since the 1950s. The very early versions took photos from space, then ejected a canister with the film inside, which was picked up as it floated back down to Earth. The film was developed into blurry photos, then examined by scientists using a magnifying glass. Later, the satellites carried digital equipment that meant the images could be sent to a computer. Today, countries can send high-quality spy satellites into space that use **infrared** and laser technology to send detailed pictures of another country's airfields, nuclear weapons factories, industrial sites, and military equipment back to base. **Radar** satellites can be used to map the world and track ships at sea, both at night and through thick cloud.

NUCLEAR THREAT

One of the biggest threats to world security is nuclear war. One way to find out how advanced a country is in developing nuclear weapons, is to obtain images and details of nuclear tests that are usually done in secret. The Pentagon is using its latest **surveillance system**, called the Space-Based Infrared System (SBIRS), to supply data of nuclear activity from other countries that may be a threat to national security.

SBIRS uses different types of space satellites and equipment to collect data and process information at control centers on the ground. SBIRS data can be used in **real time** to calculate when a nuclear missile is launched, its direction, and its possible impact, or hit points, so that it can be stopped before it reaches its target.

Film from spy satellite cameras is collected by a technician to be checked for national security risks.

A nuclear explosion can destroy cities and kill and injure thousands of people.

DARK SCIENCE SECRETS

In 1985, a space satellite was destroyed by an anti-satellite missile known as a miniature kill vehicle (MKV), fired from a U.S. Air Force fighter. It was part of a series of tests to find ways to destroy enemy satellites without breaking any of the rules of the Outer Space Treaty, a document that forms the basis of space law. The program was stopped in 1987. Anti-satellite systems have also been tested by Russia, China, and India.

13

FROM SPACE TO EARTH

The Russians launched the first space satellite—Sputnik 1—in 1957. It was about the size of a beach ball and took around 98 minutes to orbit Earth. The U.S. Navy then developed their own satellite system called TRANSIT, which they used to find enemy submarines.

In 1983, the Russians shot down a Korean **civilian**, or nonmilitary, aircraft when its pilot flew it into Russian airspace without realizing where he was. As a result of this, President Ronald Reagan said that all civilian aircraft could use the TRANSIT system for free to keep an accidental tragedy such as this from happening again. Over the years, the TRANSIT system was improved and developed, until the **Global Positioning System (GPS)** as we know it today was launched in 1989. The system is now used around the world on a variety of devices.

Developed for the military, GPS devices are now a common feature on smartphones.

SELECTIVE AVAILABILITY

Although the U.S. government allowed free use of the GPS system, they still had to protect their military bases from both civilian and military enemies overseas. As a result, the government decided to distort the signal, so that it was accurate to within only a range of about 300 feet (91 m). This was called Selective Availability (SA). In 2000, President Clinton signed an order ending SA, so that the GPS system was more useful for civilians and industry.

DARK SCIENCE SECRETS

The GPS system played a critical role in the 1991 Gulf War. U.S. troops moved into Kuwait in the Middle East to begin Operation Desert Storm, the code name for the U.S.-led army attack on Iraq. The U.S. soldiers found themselves in unfamiliar surroundings—a rocky, windy desert with no landmarks to use as guides. The soldiers used the GPS to update their route information on the battlefield. This helped them move their artillery guns and missile launchers quickly to the next battle site before the Iraqi army could reach them. Because this gave the U.S. soldiers a great advantage over the Iraqi army, it was essential that the GPS system was kept top secret. The Iraqi army believed that U.S. troops would become hopelessly lost, then they could move in and capture them. But the GPS system made sure that Operation Desert Storm was a success.

UNGUARDED

In the Gulf War, the Iraqis left wide areas of the desert unguarded—they thought that U.S. soldiers would not be able to find their way through it. However, the U.S. military had the GPS system to guide them. When the Iraqi army eventually realized that U.S. soldiers were using GPS, they placed satellite jammers on top of important buildings to keep the GPS system from locating them, so the U.S. army could not destroy them. Despite this, the war was eventually a success for the West.

The GPS system in Iraq helped keep soldiers safe and kept their vehicles from being bombed.

MAP APP ATTACK

In January 2018, it was discovered that an app using GPS was revealing the secret locations of military sites around the world. The Global Heat Map app shows locations and activities of people around the world who are using fitness devices to map where they have been running, cycling, swimming, or doing other activities over the last two years. Military experts studying the map realized that it also showed the sites of army bases around the world. These locations included those used by soldiers who had been running for exercise and using the app while on active duty in places such as Afghanistan. It was feared that the map could provide data for enemies on the location of sites that had been kept top secret.

CLASSIFIED SPACE MISSIONS

The U.S. Air Force's fourth X-37B mission finally landed at the Kennedy Space Center in 2017 after 718 days in orbit. It is one of a series of military unmanned space planes also known as Orbital Test Vehicles (OTVs). The U.S. Air Force says that the space missions were supposed to conduct experiments and test new technology that could be useful for future space missions. But the whole operation was **classified**, and details are top secret.

There have been many suggestions about what the true purpose of the X-37Bs might be. Some say they could be secret weapons that could drop bombs from space, or they are testing technology that can destroy enemy satellites or be used to spy on enemy nations.

Could superfast and powerful missiles, which are able to fire from just above Earth's orbit at targets on Earth, be a weapon of the future?

The U.S. Air Force has always denied that the X-37B is a weapon.

TOMORROW'S SECRETS

The Outer Space Treaty bans weapons of mass destruction in space, but there is plenty of **speculation** about the type of weapons that could be used from space. Satellites could be armed with weapons that could be fired at Earth. One weapon idea, called "Rods from God," is a rod-shaped missile that can be fired at Earth like a "dart from space." It would be guided to its target with complete accuracy and explode on impact with the force of a small nuclear bomb. Although the U.S. Air Force claims that it has stopped the program, some believe that the missiles are still being developed and may even have been tested under top secret conditions.

IS ANYONE OUT THERE?

What would intelligent life on other planets mean for people on Earth? It could change our lives forever. If an alien race is advanced in areas of technology and science, it could share knowledge with us, and together we could make even more advances in these areas. But aliens could also bring new diseases and a type of warfare to Earth that has never been seen before. For governments, discovering alien life could give them an advantage over all other nations, allowing them to develop new technology unknown to anyone else on the planet. If one country's government discovered alien life, would they share it with the rest of the world or keep it a secret?

ROSWELL—A GOVERNMENT COVER-UP?

In 1947, a rancher in Roswell, New Mexico, found strange metal pieces on his land that he could not identify. He took it to the local army airfield. They issued a statement saying that the debris was a "flying disk." Later, the air force said that the debris was from a weather balloon. Then, in the 1970s, unidentified flying object (UFO) followers claimed that the weather balloon story was a government **cover-up.** They said that the air force had discovered alien bodies in the wreck but was keeping it a secret. This led to the U.S. government revealing that the pieces had not come from a weather balloon but from a top secret craft used for military **surveillance**. Since then, there have been rumors of more cover-ups, more UFO sightings, and secret experiments on aliens.

The official government response is that the craft that crash-landed at Roswell was a nuclear test surveillance balloon.

With communications being sent deeper and deeper into space, there is an ever-increasing chance that we could come across intelligent alien life in the future.

TOMORROW'S SECRETS

In 2015, a program was developed called *Breakthrough Listen*. It is a ten-year program to search the universe for alien communications. The program uses **radio telescopes** based in Australia, California, and West Virginia. China is also searching deep space for **extraterrestrials** using the world's biggest radio telescope. Its potential to discover alien races is 5 to 10 times that of current equipment and will be able to reach 1 million stars. It can search deeper into space than any other telescope and spot planets that are too dark to be seen using other equipment. However, there is a general belief that any communication with an alien race would be kept secret from the general public, because it could cause panic and also have a serious impact on different religions around the world.

CHAPTER 3

RISKS AND REWARDS

The race for space is on, but only the extremely wealthy can take part. Developing space technology and science costs billions of dollars, and there is no guarantee of success. Is it worth the risk? And what profits or other rewards can be made from exploring space?

payload, the Orion spacecraft

rocket

rocket boosters

ROCKET SCIENCE

Without rockets, we could not reach space. A rocket is a powerful engine used to **thrust**, or push, payloads into space. A payload is the name given to the load or object the rocket is carrying. This might be a satellite, or a craft carrying humans or supplies to a space station. A rocket engine turns fuel into hot gas. The hot gas is then pushed out of the back of the rocket engine in a blaze of fire and smoke. This gives the rocket the power to lift up and move skyward through Earth's atmosphere. Some rockets use liquid fuel, while others use solid fuel.

A new Space Launch System (SLS) was used to thrust Orion into orbit. The exploration craft has the ability to carry humans farther into space than ever before.

20

INTO THE DARK

NASA is developing the most powerful rockets they have ever used for their next phase of space exploration. The SLS will be used to launch spacecraft into deep space to explore the Moon, Mars, and the depths of the solar system. The rockets will use a mix of both solid and liquid fuel to give them the extra power they need to push deeper into space. There are plans for the SLS to send astronauts to the Moon and Mars. It will also launch experiments into deep space that will provide important data for scientists back on Earth.

The SLS will carry several smaller craft into space, and these will be used for scientific experiments.

TOMORROW'S SECRETS

Astra Space is a company that specializes in developing smaller, cheaper next-generation rockets that it sells to other companies for huge profits. As well as making the company wealthy, it could also make it a leader in future commercial rocket sales. Astra Space had a license to test its Rocket 1 in July 2018 from Kodiak Island, Alaska. A spokesperson for Astra Space refused to give any details, saying only that they are "... very pleased with the outcome." However, the Federal Aviation Administration (FAA), which issues the license, said there was "a mishap" that they are investigating.

THE FUTURE IS PLASMA

It can take just a day to reach the Moon, but it takes about six to nine months to reach Mars. Space scientists have to find a way to keep the spacecraft powered for that length of time. This is where revolutionary **plasma** or electric rockets come in. These rockets have been developed to provide fuel for the long journey to Mars. The plasma is a mix of small **particles** called ions. The plasma is fired out from the back of the spacecraft to make the craft move forward. Plasma is not strong enough to power a rocket into space, but it can keep a spacecraft flying for much longer than any other type of fuel once the spacecraft is in space.

LAUNCH TIME

It is not only governments that are investing billions in rockets and other space technology. In 2018, the company Rocket Lab set up the world's first private launchpad with the aim of using it as a commercial business. The launchpad, based in New Zealand, had a successful test flight using its new Electron booster rocket. This small-but-powerful rocket can carry payloads into space for paying customers. The Electron rocket can carry up to 500 pounds (227 kg) into space. This is not very much compared with some of the bigger, more powerful rockets, but Rocket Lab is aiming to be a cheaper alternative to some of the companies that can carry bigger payloads.

The Electron rocket could be the space equivalent of a truck delivery service taking supplies to space stations.

If New Horizons is shattered by **space junk**, it will release deadly **plutonium** pellets into space.

DARK SCIENCE SECRETS

The New Horizons spacecraft launched by NASA in 2006 used a fuel called plutonium to power its electrical systems, so that it could reach Pluto, the most distant world explored by a spacecraft. Plutonium is very **toxic**, or poisonous, and can cause cancer and other fatal diseases. If plutonium enters Earth's atmosphere, it could create **radiation**, which would threaten life on the planet.

The plutonium pellets in the New Horizons spacecraft are protected inside layers of a superstrong material called graphite, **fiberglass insulation**, and aluminum to keep it safe from extremely high levels of heat. The pellets have been tested to remain safe during all normal conditions, including possible accidents. However, no matter how much safety testing is done, with space missions there is always a chance that something can go wrong. Although it is unlikely, there is no guarantee that there will not be a plutonium leak, and if there is, this could lead to a major disaster.

INVESTING IN SPACE

A few big aerospace companies, such as SpaceX, Blue Origin, and Virgin Galactic, are paving the way for the future of space tourism by investing massive amounts of money into new technology. The people who have built these companies believe the financial investments and risks they are taking are well worth the effort, not only financially, but for the excitement and thrill of investing in the next generation of space travel.

GAME CHANGER

A rocket can only be used once. When the payload has been launched into space, its rocket launcher falls back to Earth, where it breaks up. Some shuttle rocket launchers parachute down to Earth into the ocean, where the navy picks them up. Having to build new rockets for every space mission is one of the main reasons why space exploration is so expensive. But all this is about to change. In 2015, Jeff Bezos, the founder of Blue Origin, a business that develops space rockets, made a major breakthrough. He fired a rocket into space, then brought it safely back down to Earth in one piece. During the test, the rocket shed its payload in space, refired its engines, and slowly fell to Earth, making a safe and controlled landing.

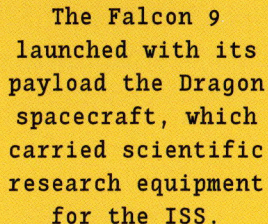

The Falcon 9 launched with its payload the Dragon spacecraft, which carried scientific research equipment for the ISS.

Space X's Falcon 9 landed on an **autonomous spaceport drone ship (ASDS)** designed to collect the rocket after launching.

CUTTING EDGE, CUTTING COSTS

In 2017, the aerospace company SpaceX launched a reused rocket called Falcon 9. The founder of SpaceX, Elon Musk, claims that reusing rockets will result in a 100 percent reduction in the cost of space travel. After its flight and return to Earth, the Falcon 9 rocket was inspected, refueled, and reused within 24 hours of landing. This quick turnaround, plus the savings in rebuilding costs, could be the key to opening up the next stage of space exploration.

DARK SCIENCE SECRETS

In 2014, Richard Branson's space company, Virgin Galactic, launched a spacecraft that crashed on a test flight, killing one of the two pilots and seriously injuring the other. An investigation said pilot error and poor safety procedures were to blame. This crash highlighted the risks pilots take and the responsibility aerospace companies have for the safety of their pilots and, eventually, the people they may one day be sending on space vacations. Engineers can prepare for all the accidents they know could happen, but until there have been flights to Mars and deeper into space, we do not know what some of the hazards might be.

MISSIONS TO MARS

Carrying tourists or large, heavy loads into space requires rockets that have the thrust to break free of **Earth's atmosphere**. Earth's atmosphere is a layer of gases held down by gravity. A rocket needs a lot of power to escape Earth's gravity. Future space exploration may include trips to Mars and beyond. These will be long journeys that require powerful rockets to push the spacecraft deeper into space. SpaceX is planning a mission to Mars in 2022. Its objective would be to find water on Mars and to identify anything that could be a danger to human life. The company also plans to build a space base for future missions. A second mission, planned for 2024, would take cargo and a crew to the red planet to start building a base that could be the basis of a future city on Mars.

HEAVY-DUTY ROCKETS

To achieve these trips to Mars, SpaceX is developing its Big Falcon Rocket (BFR), a launch vehicle that has the power to carry very heavy weights out of Earth's atmosphere and into space. The BFR will have a rocket with 31 engines and carry a spacecraft that can hold more than 100 people. It will carry up to 150 tons (136 metric tons) of cargo compared with SpaceX rockets, which carry 30 tons (27 metric tons). The rockets and spacecraft are fully reusable in a short time, making them far cheaper than any rockets or spacecraft that have been used to date.

Colonies on Mars could one day be possible thanks to the carrying power of modern rockets.

SECRET TESTS

SpaceX and Virgin Galactic are both in the race to get to Mars first and start preparing the planet for human life. The technology and science involved in their program development are often kept top secret. Flight tests are done deep in the desert away from prying eyes. When all the tests are done, there is often a grand revealing of the outcomes, such as a YouTube video, press events, and details on social media.

On Mars, people will need suits to protect them from the poisonous atmosphere and radiation. Special suits will also help people breathe.

DARK SCIENCE SECRETS

One of the many possible hazards of space travel is **contamination**—picking up unknown bacteria or diseases that astronauts could bring back to Earth. When the Apollo 11 astronauts landed on Earth after the trip to the Moon, they were kept in **quarantine** for three weeks. Quarantine is a place where people (or animals) are kept away from anyone else until scientists are sure that they do not have any illnesses that might be **infectious**. If unknown bacteria from space spread to humans, it could be devastating. The bacteria could cause illnesses we have never known before, with no known cures, possibly leading to deaths.

Humans would not be able to fight off alien bacteria brought to Earth.

CHAPTER 4

THE FUTURE IS NOW

For many years, only government organizations, such as NASA in the United States, launched astronauts into space. Today, Virgin Galactic, SpaceX, and Blue Origins are tied in the race to be the first privately owned company to take humans into deep space.

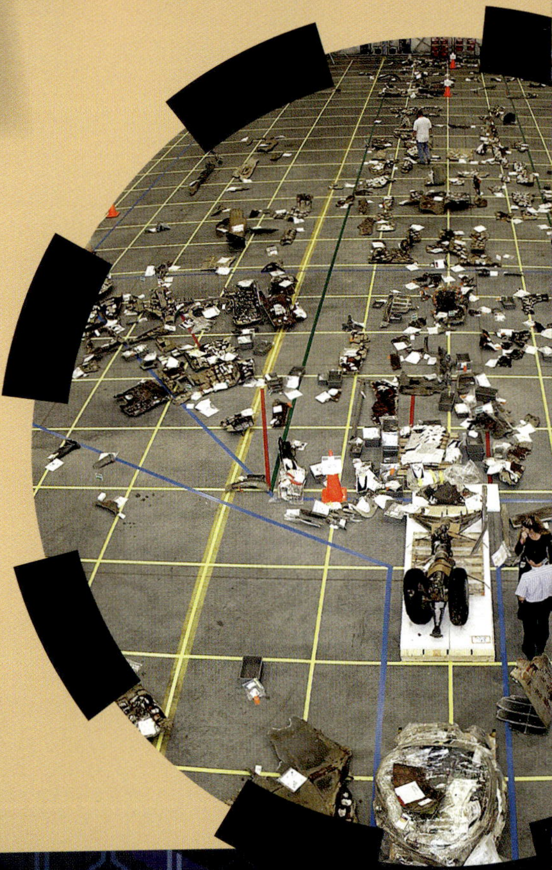

DEATH-DEFYING RETURN

The most dangerous parts of space travel are the launch and the return to Earth. A spacecraft has to hit Earth's upper atmosphere at just the right angle to keep it from plummeting down to Earth, pulled by gravity. The craft then has to be strong enough to cope with the incredible speeds of reentry—22 times the speed of sound. And the craft has to be able to protect the crew from the fierce heat caused by **friction**, a rubbing force created by gravity as the craft reenters Earth's atmosphere. There are no second chances if things go wrong.

FATAL ERRORS

Many unmanned spacecraft have broken up or exploded during missions or test flights. In 1967, three astronauts died when their Apollo 1 capsule caught fire during a routine ground test. Then, in 1986, 73 seconds after takeoff, the space shuttle Challenger turned into a fireball that killed the entire crew. Years later, in 2003, the space shuttle Columbia broke apart as it was returning to base, and again, there were no survivors. Experts have since admitted that they were aware there might have been some faults in the technology, but no one fully understood the risks involved. The accidents were, sadly, part of learning about what could go wrong.

The crew of the Columbia space shuttle were leaders in space exploration.

DARK SCIENCE SECRETS

In 2003, after a 16-day journey into space, the shuttle Columbia and its crew of seven astronauts began their reentry through Earth's atmosphere back to the NASA base. They never made it. At 200,000 feet (60,906 m) over Texas, the spacecraft completely disintegrated, and its entire crew was killed. An investigation found that during the launch, a small piece of insulation material had broken off the shuttle's outer fuel tank and had torn a hole in the wing. This meant that the craft could not survive the scorching heat of reentry. The investigation also found flaws in the design of the crew's seats, seat belts, space suits, and **life-support systems**. As a result of this devastating accident and the investigation, NASA has improved its safety procedures and equipment.

Thousands of pieces of the space shuttle Columbia were collected to find out what had caused the accident.

SPACE SUITS OF THE FUTURE

Boeing's CST-100 Starliner is the latest design in space capsules that will transport humans and cargo to the ISS. It can be reused up to ten times with a six-month turnaround time. Cutting-edge space suits have been designed for the astronauts who will fly in the Starliner.

The Starliner suits are lightweight and designed for easy movement. Each suit will be made to perfectly fit individual crew members, for their maximum comfort and safety. Special meshing at the elbow and shoulder joints will make it easier for astronauts to use their arms. The astronauts will wear lightweight leather gloves, so they can use touch screens on computers and tablets onboard—something that was not necessary for the first astronauts, because digital devices had not been invented at that time.

An astronaut is fitted for her Starliner suit to make sure it is comfortable and works correctly.

TOMORROW'S ASTRONAUTS

The Orion is the latest spacecraft designed to take astronauts deep into space, thousands of miles beyond the Moon. In the future, it could fly to asteroids and Mars. The six-month-or-longer journey to Mars will put a lot of pressure on astronauts physically and mentally. They will be living in a small area and could suffer from feelings of **isolation** as they travel millions of miles away from Earth and everything they know. They will then face harsh living conditions on Mars when they arrive at the planet.

Space suits and equipment made for missions to Mars are tested in the Sun-scorched Mojave Desert.

TOUGH TRAINING

Astronauts traveling into deep space need special skills to survive and have to go through tough training. NASA and the European Space Agency (ESA) are now training astronauts for life on Mars. This consists of three phases. In phase one, crew members will have medical training or learn how to use and repair equipment and solve technical problems. They will have to learn about **geology** and **exobiology,** the biology of alien life. Phase two will test how well they can cope with living for a long time in a small space, without any face-to-face time with family and friends. Phase three will be months of **simulation** training—living exactly as they would on the long, lonely, and dangerous flight through space.

TOMORROW'S SECRETS

Reentry into Earth's atmosphere is still a crucial danger point. As we have seen, in the past the craft Columbia broke up on reentry and astronauts died. The Starliner is using a new parachute system to make sure the space capsule lands safely. In the first test, the drop down took four minutes and reached speeds of 300 miles per hour (482 kph) before the capsule landed gently on the ground. Tests will continue, and top space scientists and engineers will analyze the results before the launch gets the go-ahead. However, there is always the risk that something could go wrong. Another deadly accident could set back the NASA space program for a very long time.

RESERVE YOUR PLACE IN SPACE

Wealthy businesspeople and Hollywood stars are already booking their vacations and journeys into space. This could be a quick trip around the planet, a visit to a space station in **low Earth orbit (LEO)**, which is about 1,200 miles (1,930 km) above Earth, or a permanent stay on Mars. Private citizens have already started to pay for trips to the ISS, which reportedly cost from $20 million to $40 million. Private companies are building space stations, which will travel in LEO and be used for vacations, or rented to governments, scientists, or other businesses.

SPACESHIPTWO-AGAIN!

Virgin Galactic developed SpaceShipTwo for its space tourism program. But after the deadly crash in 2014, when one of the pilots was killed on a test flight, the program was temporarily put on hold. After years spent improving the design faults that caused the accident in 2014, Virgin Galactic completed a successful test flight with its latest space tourism spacecraft, *Unity*. Following this success, the company plans to start **suborbital** flights into low Earth space within the year. Suborbital flights go straight up into space just above Earth's surface, then come straight down again. On a flight like this, tourists would experience three to six minutes of weightlessness and see the curve of Earth against the darkness of space.

Unity had a successful test flight, but any missions into space can still be dangerous.

WHAT IF SOMETHING GOES WRONG?

Astronauts train for years before they travel into space. Space tourists may have to undergo a few months of training for long journeys—but nothing for short, suborbital flights. No one knows what the impact of long journeys in tiny capsules shared with strangers might have on a person's mental or physical health. What happens if there is a crisis—if someone has a heart attack or a panic attack, or if there is a technical failure? A space tourist would be trapped far away from help in an alien environment. Another danger could be a collision with space junk. There are thousands of pieces of space trash floating around that could cause serious damage. In space, there are no emergency services to come to the rescue.

Travelers in the space hotel Aurora Station will have three months of space training. Usually, it is 24 months!

TOMORROW'S SECRETS

There are no national or international safety standards on space tourism vehicles as there are with airplanes. At the moment, space tourists sign a piece of paper saying that they acknowledge there might be dangers and accept all risks. Also, because there is such rivalry between private space companies, they are often reluctant to discuss their technology and engineering developments in case ideas are stolen. This means that safety risks for travelers are not being discussed openly, and people who sign up for space travel may not be aware of all the possible risks they are taking.

CHAPTER 5

LIVING IN SPACE

As the population on Earth increases, so the race to find ways to live on Mars or elsewhere in space has become more urgent. Perhaps we could live on space stations or in space cities and float among stars—or **colonize** a passing asteroid?

EARTH TO SPACE STATION

People already live in space. The ISS is the biggest object ever flown in space. It orbits 199 miles (320 km) above Earth. It has 16 huge **solar panels**, devices that use sunlight to create energy, and several sections in which astronauts live and work. There is also a huge science laboratory where astronauts can perform experiments in weightless conditions. Automated Transfer Vehicles (ATVs) take supplies to the ISS from Earth.

> The ISS can be seen from Earth as it travels around the planet 16 times a day. Onboard, astronauts have to cope with living in a place where there is no up or down.

FREE FALL

In Earth's orbit, astronauts experience weightlessness. This can be fun, but it has serious health issues. Without gravity, blood and other bodily fluids flow toward the head. This can cause headaches and make people feel groggy and stuffed up. Pushing against gravity keeps our bones and muscles strong, so without this, people would need to exercise every day for several hours. Some may need to wear special pants that pull blood to the legs and make the heart pump faster. In space, without normal day and night patterns, natural body rhythms such as sleep times become unbalanced, and this can be harmful mentally and physically.

> In space, everything has to be tied down, including people! What is not secured will float around in zero gravity.

NO WATER

There is very little water in space, so water has to be delivered from Earth. Plus, water floats in the air. There are no showers, so everyone just has a sponge bath with a damp cloth. The toilet uses air to flush instead of water. Urine is made clean and recycled. Many space suits are fitted with diapers!

TOMORROW'S SECRETS

Ark 1 is a space habitat being designed by the Lifeboat Foundation, an organization developing cutting-edge technology. It is being developed to rescue survivors from a future worldwide disaster. The craft will be **self-sufficient**, so that it does not rely on anything from Earth. It will have artificial gravity and an artificial ecosystem that will allow plants and animals to grow and survive in space. It will use resources such as water from the Moon and asteroids. No one outside of the Foundation really knows how Ark 1 will work, but the scientists and engineers putting the Ark together say that it could save humankind if there is a catastrophic disaster on Earth.

SPACE GARDEN

NASA is already experimenting with growing food in space. On the ISS, astronauts have been growing lettuce, peas, and radishes in their "space garden." Growing their own food from seeds obviously means that less food has to be transported from Earth and that space dwellers will have fresh—not just prepackaged—food to eat. Looking after a garden and growing vegetables is also good for mental health. It helps the crew relax and feel more like they are back home on Earth.

Growing food in colonies on Mars and space cities will make them self-sufficient and able to supply their own food. Eating fresh vegtables will be healthier and make it feel more like home.

PRINTING IN SPACE

When equipment on the ISS goes wrong or needs repairing, spare parts and tools such as screws, clamps, and wrenches are delivered by an ATV. But now, the ISS has printed its first **three-dimensional (3-D)** object in space using a 3-D printer. This means that spacecraft can now travel deeper into space and stay away longer because they will not rely on craft from Earth to supply them with tools and essential equipment. Crews in space can now ask for a picture of the object they need to be emailed to them. The printer will then make the object. The 3-D printers work by **extruding**, or squeezing out, plastic layers that build up the 3-D object.

Coffee from a real cup can help space travelers enjoy the drink more. It is more natural than drinking from a sealed bag and a straw.

SPACE CUPS

Today, drinking in space is done through straws out of sealed bags, so that liquid does not escape and float around. This means that astronauts do not enjoy the full flavor or smell of the drinks. A company is now developing cups that can be used in space. Apart from making the drinking experience more enjoyable, this can cut down on the amount of cargo that has to be taken onboard, and as drink bags are not reusable, it reduces trash.

TOMORROW'S SECRETS

3-D printing in space has led to a race to build in space. NASA is developing printers that could use the grit on the surface of Mars to print bricks to build shelters. The ESA is using dust on the Moon to make bricks to build a Moon base. The first organization or company to print building materials in space will be able to lead the way in colonizing other planets such as Mars. It will be able to build places for people to live and work on distant planets.

DANGEROUS JOURNEY

A lot of research is being done into how humans can live on Mars. But how easy will life on the red planet really be? The first challenge will be to get to Mars, and the journey will be filled with danger. Earth's atmosphere protects us from harmful rays from the Sun, but in space and on Mars, there is no protection. **Solar flares** fired from the Sun's surface could wipe out electrical equipment and deliver deadly doses of radiation. **Meteorites** smashing into spacecraft could also pose a serious threat. Once Mars is reached, landing could be tricky. To date, there have been only seven successful landings on the red planet.

SLEEP ALL THE WAY

SpaceWorks is an aerospace engineering firm that investigates the possibility of putting travelers to Mars into a sleeplike state for the whole journey. They claim this can help lower health risks, such as a person's bones becoming weaker, and will also reduce consumption of supplies such as food. Once travelers arrive at Mars and wake up, what would be next?

```
Solar flares could
cause people living in
space to get radiation
sickness, leading to
vomiting, exhaustion,
and blood problems.
```

The first people on Mars could be involved in researching how to grow food on a planet where there is less pressure and less sunlight than on Earth.

LIFE ON MARS

There is no oxygen on Mars, it is freezing cold, sandstorms are blinding, the soil is toxic, and exposure to radiation is a constant threat. But Mars is the second most **habitable** planet in our solar system, so businesses and governments are looking at ways to make life on Mars possible for humans. Water on Mars can be sourced and made pure for drinking, and the toxic soil can be **decontaminated** and used to grow food.

With the development of 3-D printing, people in space colonies or cities do not need to rely on supplies from Earth. Another plus for those living in space is the development of space suits that are lighter, more comfortable, give better protection, and are quicker to get on and off.

TOMORROW'S SECRETS

The first humans may find it difficult to adapt to the harsh conditions on Mars. But for future generations, life could be made easier by **terraforming** Mars. This means changing a planet so that it is able to support human life. If the atmosphere was made thicker and the temperature raised, plants could grow there. Plants would release oxygen into the air, so humans might be able to breathe the air on Mars without using a mask or suit.

Medical scientists are not sure what long-term effects low gravity over months and years might have on humans. It could shorten their lives, or it could make them live longer. The exploration of space is exciting, but the risks are unknown.

CHAPTER 6
WHAT NEXT?

The future of space exploration is very exciting. What was once science fiction could well become "science fact" in the next 20 years, such as landing people on Mars and mining asteroids. To keep up with the race for space, industries and professions involved in science, technology, and engineering will have to advance their knowledge quickly, so that they are not left behind.

MAKING LIVES BETTER

The funding used for space programs is providing new products that are helping a lot of people in their everyday lives. For example, improved artificial limbs, lifesaving heart pumps, longer-lasting tires, and cordless vacuum cleaners, are all based on technology originally developed for space programs. So, too, are freeze-drying techniques for preprepared meals, better quality baby foods, and firefighting equipment widely used throughout the United States.

Did you know that the thermometer that takes the temperature in your ear was first developed for astronauts?

TRASH AND CRASH

There is a lot of junk in orbital space, and it travels at such high speeds that a piece the size of a marble could cause the ISS serious damage. At NASA headquarters, ground control scientists constantly monitor the ISS looking for pieces of junk nearby that could damage the station and be a threat to the lives of the crew onboard. This has already happened several times, but luckily, all have been near misses. The U.S. Air Force Command tracks around 22,000 pieces of human-made space junk that are bigger than 2 inches (5 cm) wide. There are hundreds of thousands of smaller pieces floating around, but those are difficult to track.

If ground controllers see a piece of debris heading for the ISS, they warn the crew to take shelter.

TOMORROW'S SECRETS

There are many ideas in development for how to clean up space, such as using giant magnets, nets, harpoons, and powerful laser light beams. Scientists in China have been developing the idea of a powerful laser based in space that would push dangerous pieces of junk into Earth's atmosphere. There, they would burn up or could be pushed out of the way of a collision with the space station. However, there are concerns that such a laser could also be used as a weapon to destroy enemy satellites or space stations.

Meteorites hurtling toward spacecraft could be shattered by lasers into smaller pieces that would then harmlessly burn up in Earth's atmosphere.

SPACE COLONIES

As the population on Earth grows, we need more housing. However, building new homes takes up farmland that is needed to produce more food to feed the growing population. Our planet is becoming too crowded, and our **resources** such as fuel, water, and food are running out. One solution is to move, but to where? Space colonies, such as cities in space, may be one answer.

THE LONG SLEEP

Traveling in a sleeplike state will overcome the problem of what to do during the months or even years of being forced to live in a small spacecraft. It could also lead the way for even longer space trips, for example, to Jupiter, which could take five years to reach from Earth. Travelers would be fed through a tube and monitored regularly. However, the body's muscles become weak when they are not used regularly, so more research would have to be done to overcome this.

Small pods, such as these, could be home for sleeping humans as they travel through deep space for many years.

Could the people on a generation spaceship (see below) **evolve**, or change, into a new species of human that can live and thrive in deepest space?

CONTAMINATION

There is also the threat of contamination: that something from space may contaminate Earth and humans, or that humans may contaminate something in space. There are also concerns that rock and earth samples the astronauts bring back from space for testing in labs on Earth might be contaminated by humans, which will make the experiments worthless.

TOMORROW'S SECRETS

Many space ideas, such as life on Mars, started in the minds of writers, and now scientists and engineers are trying to make them a reality. A generation spaceship is one that travels for hundreds or thousands of years through deep space to find a star system or planet that humans could colonize. How would humans adjust to living their entire lives in a spacecraft? Would it lead to a new race of humans who only know how to live in dark space? What would the mental effect be on humans used to living on Earth? It may be many years before we have the knowledge to make a generation ship a reality, but we know that what some people can imagine in stories and movies, others can make happen in real life.

43

BE A SPACE EXPLORER

We have seen how science and technology are making space travel possible. Imagine that you own an aerospace company. What would be the main mission of your company—to travel to Mars, mine an asteroid, explore deeper into space, or begin a human colony on another planet?

YOUR MISSION

- Research what you would need to be able to survive on your chosen mission. Find out about the atmosphere, gravity, food, minerals, and water of where you plan to live.

- Write a mission statement saying where you are going and why. Is it to make a profit, to help humankind if there is a disaster on Earth, for adventure, or to discover if there is other life in the universe?

- What already exists that could help you on your mission?

- What new tools or new technology would you have to develop to make your mission a success?

- Would you be willing to share any new technology that you develop with other companies?

- Would you go on the mission into space or stay on Earth? Explain your decision.

Space is vast and unknown. How would you protect your mission against the dangers of outer space?

TOP SECRET

How would you guard your space secrets, and what dark science might come about as a result of your investigations? If something went terribly wrong, would you keep it a secret or share your knowledge with the world?

GLOSSARY

Please note: Some **bold-faced** words are defined where they appear in the book.

ABMs Short for anti-ballistic missiles, which intercept and destroy missiles

asteroids Rocky objects in space, usually found between Mars and Jupiter

atmosphere The "blanket" of gases surrounding a planet

autonomous spaceport drone ship (ASDS) A rocket landing pad at sea without any crew

civilian Not part of the armed forces

classified Secret and to be seen only by approved people

colonies Groups of people living together in one place

colonize To settle permanently in a place and take ownership of it

contamination Something that makes something else poisoned or impure

decontaminated Made clean or pure

electrodes Conductors that are usually metal and used to transfer electricity to things that are not metal

electronic jammers Radio signals used to interfere with the signals coming from a satellite

extraterrestrials Beings from outer space; aliens

fiberglass An extremely strong material made from lots of thin threads of glass

geology The study of rocks

Global Positioning System (GPS) A navigation system that uses signals from satellites to find the location of a radio receiver on or above Earth

gravity The force that draws objects toward one another

habitable Suitable to live in or on

infectious Easily spread

infrared A type of invisible light that feels warm

insulation A material used to keep an object's temperature constant

International Space Station (ISS) A space station in low Earth orbit with a crew that conducts research and experiments

isolation Separate from others

lasers Intense beams of light

life-support systems Systems that provide everything an organism needs to stay alive, such as oxygen and water

meteorites Pieces of rock or metal that fall to Earth from space

military To do with the army

monitor To watch carefully

national security The safety of a country

nuclear Connected to nuclear energy

orbit The path an object takes as it travels around a star, planet, or moon

particles Tiny pieces

plasma A type of gas

plutonium A radioactive material used in nuclear weapons

radar A device that uses radio signals to find the location of objects

radiation A type of heat energy

radio telescopes Instruments used to pick up radio signals from space

real time The actual time when something is happening

reentry Coming through Earth's atmosphere from space to land on Earth

satellites Human-made objects that orbit Earth, usually used to gather information or for communication

signal scramblers Devices used to distort or change a signal coming from a satellite or other electronic device

solar flares Enormous explosions of energy from the Sun's surface

space junk Human-made objects, such as old satellites and pieces of spacecraft, that have broken up in space

speculation Talking about possible outcomes

surveillance Closely watching a place or person to gather information

surveillance system A television system used to watch a place or person

three-dimensional (3-D) Having three dimensions—height, width, and length

LEARNING MORE

BOOKS

Aguilar, A. David. *Space Encyclopedia: A Tour of Our Solar System and Beyond* (National Geographic Kids). National Geographic Children's Books, 2013.

Aldrin, Buzz, with Marianne J. Dyson. *Welcome to Mars: Making a Home on the Red Planet* (Science and Nature). National Geographic Children's Books, 2015.

Jefferis, David. *Space Explorers: From Earth to Infinity* (Our Future in Space). Crabtree Publishing, 2017.

Jefferis, David. *Space Tourists: Vacations Across the Universe* (Our Future in Space). Crabtree Publishing, 2017.

WEBSITES

http://kinooze.com/asteroid-mining-will-begin-soon
Find out more about asteroid mining and how it might work.

https://mars.nasa.gov/participate/funzone
Discover news, games, activities, and much more in this fun and interactive site all about the explorations of Mars.

www.nasa.gov/audience/forstudents/k-4/home/F_Living_in_Space.html
Find out how astronauts live and work in space.

www.nationalgeographic.com/science/space/space-exploration/future-spaceflight
Learn about the future of space exploration by aerospace companies and NASA.

INDEX

3-D printing 36, 37, 39

Aldrin, Buzz 8
alien bacteria 27
aliens 18-19, 31
antiballistic missiles (ABMs) 9
Ark 1 35
Armstrong, Neil 8
asteroids 6, 7, 8, 30, 35, 40
Automated Transfer Vehicles (ATVs) 34

Big Falcon Rocket (BFR) 26

Challenger 29
colonies 8, 26, 36, 39, 42
Columbia 29, 31
contamination 27, 43

electron rocket 22
European Space Agency (ESA) 31
exobiology 31
extraterrestrials 19

generation spaceship 43

gravity 5, 26, 28, 35, 39, 44

International Space Station (ISS) 6, 25, 30, 32, 34, 36, 41

Kennedy Space Center 11, 16

Laika 5
low Earth orbit (LEO) 32

Mars 6, 8, 21, 22, 25, 26, 27, 30, 31, 32, 34, 36, 37, 38, 39, 40, 43, 44
meteorites 38, 41
miniature kill vehicle (MKV) 13
Moon, the 2, 4, 6, 8, 21, 22, 27, 30, 35, 37

National Aeronautics and Space Administration (NASA) 6, 21, 23, 28, 29, 31, 36, 37, 41
Near-Earth Objects (NEOs) 7
New Horizons 23

Orbital Test Vehicles (OTVs) 16
Orion (spacecraft) 20, 30
Outer Space Treaty 13, 17

Rocket 1 21
Roswell 18
Russia 4, 5, 8, 9, 10, 13

satellites 7, 8, 9, 10, 12, 13, 16, 41
Space-Based Infrared System (SBIRS) 13
space junk 23, 33, 41
Space Launch System (SLS) 20, 21
space race 4, 6, 7, 40
space suits 29, 30, 35, 39
SpaceShipTwo 32
Starliner 30, 31
suborbital flights 32, 33

terraforming 39
TRANSIT system 14

*U*nity 32

X-37B 16, 17

ABOUT THE AUTHOR
Honor Head has worked in children's publishing for many years as an editor and author. When she is not working, she enjoys being by the seaside, wondering what space journey she would choose.

48